Camp Ghost-Away

YOUNG YEARLING BOOKS YOU WILL ENJOY:

The Pee Wee Scout books by Judy Delton

COOKIES AND CRUTCHES
CAMP GHOST-AWAY
LUCKY DOG DAYS
BLUE SKIES, FRENCH FRIES
GRUMPY PUMPKINS
PEANUT-BUTTER PILGRIMS
A PEE WEE CHRISTMAS

YEARLING BOOKS/YOUNG YEARLINGS/YEARLING CLAS-SICS are designed especially to entertain and enlighten young people. Patricia Reilly Giff, consultant to this series, received the bachelor's degree from Marymount College. She holds the master's degree in history from St. John's University, and a Professional Diploma in Reading from Hofstra University. She was a teacher and reading consultant for many years, and is the author of numerous books for young readers.

For a complete listing of all Yearling titles, write
to
Dell Readers Service, P.O. Box 1045,
South Holland, IL 60473.

Camp
Ghost-Away

JUDY DELTON

Illustrated by Alan Tiegreen

A YOUNG YEARLING BOOK

For Jamie, Bandy, James, and Jim,
No matter who, I worship him.

Published by
Dell Publishing
a division of
The Bantam Doubleday Dell Publishing Group, Inc.
1 Dag Hammarskjold Plaza
New York, New York 10017

Text copyright © 1988 by Judy Delton
Illustrations copyright © 1988 by Alan Tiegreen

Yearling ® TM 913705, Dell Publishing, a division of the Bantam Doubleday Dell Publishing Group, Inc.

ISBN: 0-440-40062-7

Printed in the United States of America

July 1988

10 9 8 7

W

Contents

1 A Mountain of Donuts   7
2 The Pee Wee Spirit   17
3 Are We Almost There?   22
4 Tiny Is a Hero   34
5 Rat's Knees!   42
6 I Want My Mother   54
7 Molly the Brave   62
8 Badges   73

CHAPTER 1

A Mountain of Donuts

At last it was Tuesday. Tuesday was Pee Wee Scout Day. It took forever for Tuesday to come, thought Molly Duff.

Soon Troop 23 stood around the Scout table at Mrs. Peters's house. On the table were boxes and boxes of Scout donuts.

They were piled up like a mountain. A mountain of donuts. They had powdered sugar on them, like snow. Snow on the mountain, thought Molly.

Molly rubbed her stomach. She wished the Scouts could eat them. Eat the whole mountain.

"Now pay attention!" called Mrs. Peters. Mrs. Peters was their troop leader.

"Today we begin to sell our donuts. You'll go door to door on your own block. We must be very polite to people," said Mrs. Peters. "Even if they don't want to buy our donuts."

But they all will, thought Molly.

"We must count the money and give them the right change. And you have to be careful not to lose the money." Mrs. Peters explained everything to the Scouts so that they would know what to do. They all listened carefully. They were eager to get started.

8

"How much do they cost?" asked Sonny Betz.

"The donuts are one dollar a box," said Mrs. Peters. "Tell the people the money is for our trip to camp. If we sell enough donuts, our whole troop will go to Pee Wee Scout camp!"

All the Scouts cheered, "Yeah!"

"And the one who sells the most donuts will get an award," said Mrs. Peters. "It will be a special Scout badge. Are there any questions?"

Molly crossed her fingers. She didn't like questions. Questions took forever.

Rachel's hand went up. She always asked questions. Mrs. Peters called on Rachel. "Mrs. Peters, my mom says we should sell something that is more healthy.

Donuts have sugar. Sugar isn't good for your teeth."

A hex on Rachel's mother. Rachel's father was a dentist. Molly loved donuts.

"Donuts are all right if you don't eat too many, Rachel," said Mrs. Peters.

Before Rachel could say anything else and before any more questions, Mrs. Peters said, "Let's get out there and sell donuts! Let's sell enough to go to Pee Wee Scout camp!"

Troop 23 dashed for the door. Each Scout held a mountain of donuts. "I am going to sell the most!" said Molly.

"I am," said Lisa Ronning. "I am going to ask my grandma to buy some."

Molly wished that her grandma lived nearby. It was too far to go to sell donuts to her grandma. She would have to sell donuts to her own block.

"I'm going to sell a million donuts," said Rachel. Rachel always had to do better than anyone else. Even if donuts were bad for your teeth.

"You can't sell a million," scoffed Roger White. "Nobody can sell a million."
"I can," said Rachel.

"I'm going to go around a lot of blocks," said Sonny Betz. "Not just my own."
"Is your mama going with you?" Rachel called out.

Everyone knew Sonny was a mama's boy. He couldn't even walk to school alone. Lots of kids called Sonny a sissy. "So what if she is?" said Sonny.

"Mama's boy, mama's boy!" shouted Rachel.

"Stuck up, stuck up!" returned Sonny.

"Let's sell donuts together," said Mary Beth Kelly to Molly. "It would be more fun, and we could go to more houses."

"Okay," said Molly.

When they got near their own block, Molly said, "Let's start here."

Mary Beth looked at the old house. A window was broken, and the paint was peeling.

"Mrs. Olson lives there," said Mary Beth. "She's mean. She doesn't like kids in her yard."

They kept walking to the next house. "Mrs. Cox is mean too," said Mary Beth.

13

*　　*　　*

"I'm going to the door anyway," said Molly bravely. She marched up to the door and knocked. An old lady came to the door.

"Do you want to buy some Scout donuts" asked Molly, "so we can go to camp?"

"I don't like donuts," said Mrs. Cox, slamming the door. Molly wanted to put a hex on Mrs. Cox, but she remembered what Mrs. Peters had said. Be polite even if they say no.

They went to the next house. Mary Beth went to the door. "Do you want to buy some Pee Wee donuts?" she asked.

"I have no teeth," said the old man who came to the door.

"You don't need teeth to eat these," said Mary Beth politely.

But he closed the door and did not answer.

The next person was not home. And the next man told them that he makes his own donuts.

"This is not as easy as I thought," said Molly. "We may never get to camp." She sighed.

Mary Beth sighed too.

They went to the last house on the block. A mother with three children came to the door. "Why, I'll take four boxes!" she said. "Two from each of you. We love donuts for dessert."

She gave the girls four dollars. "Have fun at camp!" she called.

CHAPTER 2
The Pee Wee Spirit

Molly and Mary Beth sold donuts all week long. They sold ten boxes each, and then they went back to ask Mrs. Peters for more donuts. By the next Tuesday they had each sold twelve boxes.

At three o'clock Molly went to Mary Beth's house. Then they walked to the Scout meeting together.

Everyone was turning in their donut money. Lisa Ronning turned in five dollars. Tim Noon turned in one dollar. Roger

White had sold sixteen boxes! But Sonny Betz and Rachel Myers had sold over one hundred boxes each!

"Wow!" said Molly. "There aren't even one hundred people on a whole block."

"That is really the Pee Wee spirit," said Mrs. Peters. "I think we should all clap for Sonny and Rachel!"

Everyone clapped their hands together, and shouted and whistled. Roger blew into his brown lunch bag. Then he punched it and the bag exploded. Pow!

Molly did not clap. She did not feel like cheering. She wanted to win.

"Maybe Rachel and Sonny will tell us how they sold so many donuts," said Mrs. Peters.

"My mom sold about eighty boxes at work," said Sonny proudly.

"Your mom!" shouted Roger. "That isn't

fair. You're supposed to sell them your-
self!"

Leave it to Sonny, thought Molly, to
let his mom do it. Big baby!

"What's the matter with my mom selling them?" asked Sonny. Mrs. Peters said
it was all right to have your mother sell
your donuts.

"It doesn't matter who sells them," said
Mrs. Peters. "The more boxes that are
sold, the more money for Scout camp."

"Baby Sonny," muttered Roger.

"Now, Rachel, how did you sell so
many donuts?" asked Mrs. Peters.

"I sold them to my relatives," said Rachel, with her chin in the air. "We went
to a wedding, and my aunt and my
grandma bought twenty boxes each."

All of Rachel's family must be rich,
thought Molly.

"What will they do with all those donuts?" asked Mary Beth.

"They'll get fat!" shouted Molly, filling her cheeks with air. "They'll turn into donuts if they eat twenty boxes!"

Molly waddled across the floor, pretending to be Rachel's fat relatives.

Rachel looked very angry. Her face got red. "My grandma and my aunt are not fat!" she cried.

"They will be when they finish all those donuts," said Roger, holding his sides and chuckling.

"They aren't eating the donuts themselves," said Rachel. "They will give them to hungry people."

"The main thing is that we have enough money for camp," said Mrs. Peters. "And Rachel and Sonny get the award and the best donut seller's badge."

After Scouts, Molly said to Rachel, "You didn't sell a million boxes anyway. You said you were going to sell a million."

"Well, I sold a lot more than you," said Rachel. "Your dumb twelve boxes."

Molly couldn't argue with that. She wished a hex on Rachel's aunt and grandma. And on Sonny's mom. But she was glad that the Pee Wee Scouts (and their relatives) had earned enough for them to go to camp.

CHAPTER 3

Are We Almost There?

The next Tuesday, Troop 23 met again. Mrs. Peters talked about Camp Hide-Away. She told them what to bring. She told them what to wear. And she sent notes home to their mothers with the address and telephone number of the camp.

"We will leave Friday afternoon from the school," Mrs. Peters said. "We will ride to camp in a bus. We will come home on Sunday evening."

* * *

Lisa's mother was coming along to help Mrs. Peters.

During the rest of the meeting the Scouts told good deeds they had done.

"I watered Mrs. Johnson's plants for her," said Tracy Barnes. "She's my next-door neighbor."

"I washed my dad's car," boasted Roger. "All by myself."

"Good for you!" said Mrs. Peters.

It was a short meeting. The Scouts sang their Pee Wee Scout song. Then they said the Pee Wee Scout pledge. Then they ran home to tell their parents about Camp Hide-Away.

"I've got a new swimsuit to take to camp," said Mary Beth at the park the next day. Some of the Pee Wees played there in the summer.

"I have a new swimsuit for camp too,"

called Molly from the top of the jungle gym.

"I've got two swimsuits," said Rachel. "My mom says everyone should have two. In case one is wet and you want to go in the water again."

Molly hung upside down by her knees. She tried to think of a worse word than hex. Molly learned "hex" from her grandma, but it wasn't really bad. She wanted a really bad word to use on Rachel's mother. Her mother was probably a show-off just like Rachel.

"I'm wearing my new bracelet to camp too," said Rachel. She held out her arm. "It is fourteen karat gold."

Rachel's bracelet sparkled in the sun. It looked very expensive. "My dad brought it back from New York with him," said Rachel.

*   *   *

Molly had a bracelet. But it was too small. And it was not real gold. It made her wrist turn green.

Rachel kept waving her arm so the bracelet would sparkle in Molly's eyes. Molly watched her. She wished the bracelet were hers.

The Pee Wees played in the park until suppertime. The next day they went there again. They had to wait and wait until Friday.

They ran under the sprinkler at Molly's house to make the time go faster.

They rode their skateboards in Roger's driveway to make the time go faster.

And they made lemonade at Lisa's, and tried to sell it on her front lawn, to make the time go faster. They sold only two cups. One to Lisa's mother. And one to her little brother. But he couldn't pay because he had lost his penny.

At last Friday came. All the Pee Wee Scouts carried their camp bags to the school. The school was closed, but the bus was waiting! Mrs. Peters and Mrs. Ronning were waiting too. Everyone got on the bus. Even Mrs. Peters's big black dog.

"He is coming along as our mascot," said Mrs. Peters. "His name is Tiny. He will be a watchdog in camp at night."

"Tiny!" shouted Tim. "His name should be Giant. Why would such a big dog be called Tiny?"

"Sometimes you call things the opposite of what they really are," explained Mrs. Peters. "Like sometimes if a man has no hair, they call him Curly."

The Scouts looked puzzled.

Then Roger said, "My uncle is real tall and everybody calls him Shorty!"

"That's right," said Mrs. Peters. "The opposite of what he is."

As the bus rolled along, the Scouts sang camp songs. They sang the Pee Wee Scout song too.

Mary Beth showed Molly her new swimsuit. And her new birthstone ring she got for her birthday. "Emerald," she said. "For May."

Rachel dangled her bracelet in front of everyone's eyes. Mary Beth's ring was almost as shiny.

"I don't feel so good," said Sonny. His face looked white. He leaned back in his seat and closed his eyes. He was sitting next to Lisa.

"OOOOOOoooo," he moaned, holding his stomach. "I think I'm carsick."

*   *   *

Lisa leaned over into the aisle. She didn't want to sit too close to Sonny. He might have an accident. All over her.

Sonny groaned again, and the driver stopped the bus. He took Sonny off the bus until he felt better. But Sonny's face was still white when he got back on.

The Scouts looked out the windows.

They watched the trees and telephone poles whiz by.

"How much longer?" asked Mary Beth.
"Are we almost there?" asked Roger.

Just when the ride was getting boring and Roger and Sonny began to fight, Mrs. Peters said, "Here we are!"

Tiny began to bark. The bus squealed to a stop. The Pee Wees hurried to get off.

There were tall pine trees everywhere. There was a sparkly blue lake too. And right in the middle of the dark woods stood the tents.

"Do we have to sleep in a *tent*?" whined Rachel. "I thought there would be a hotel or something."

*   *   *

Roger laughed.

Sonny cracked up.

Even Mrs. Peters smiled. "This is a camp, Rachel. Camping is living outside, close to nature."

"Ugh, bugs," said Rachel, making a face.

"Bears!" said Roger. "Not just bugs!"

Rachel screamed. "Are there bears, Mrs. Peters?"

"There could be," she said. "But we are safe with Tiny. And we must not leave food outside."

Rachel looked as if she wanted to get back on the bus and go home.

"Scaredy cat," said Molly.

"Sissy," called the boys.

Four Scouts stayed in each tent. Mrs. Peters and Mrs. Ronning were not far

31

away. Tiny stayed in Molly's tent. And Mary Beth, Rachel, and Lisa. Each Scout had a cot and a sleeping bag.

After supper, Mrs. Peters and the Pee Wees built a campfire. Everyone held hands and sang around the campfire.

The fire made shadows in the woods. The moonlight shone on the lake. It was very pretty at camp. But it was scary, too, thought Molly.

The campfire burned low. Then it went out. Mrs. Peters led the Scouts in the Pee Wee Scout pledge. Everyone held hands while they said it. They always did that when they said the pledge.

Lisa's mother and Mrs. Peters helped the Scouts get tucked into the sleeping bags for the night. Then they went to their own tent.

"It's so quiet," said Lisa.

It was quiet. Except for the wind whistling around the tent, there wasn't a sound.

And it was dark. Pitch black, dark!

"I'm not scared, are you?" whispered Mary Beth.

"Naw," said Molly. But her voice sounded like it was shaking.

"We've got Tiny and Mrs. Peters and Lisa's mother to protect us," said Mary Beth with a quiver.

And then, just when they decided to be brave, they heard a loud ghostlike sound.

"OOOOOOOOOooooooooooooo," the ghost moaned. It sounded as if it were right outside their tent!

33

CHAPTER 4

Tiny Is a Hero

"What was that?" said Molly, leaping up from her cot. The other girls sat up. Mary Beth's eyes were wide open and as big as saucers. They all listened. They had goose bumps on their arms. But all they could hear now was the wind roaring in the trees.

"It was probably just an animal," said Lisa bravely. Lisa's mother was nearby. But not close enough, thought Lisa.

"What kind of animal makes a ghost noise?" asked Rachel.

"A wild animal," said Mary Beth, rolling her eyes toward the tent door.

"A wild animal!" yelled Rachel. "I want to go home! A wild animal could eat us! A wild animal is more dangerous than a ghost!"

Molly didn't know which was more dangerous. She didn't know if she would rather meet a ghost or a tiger. A ghost, she decided. No, a tiger, she thought, changing her mind.

"It's gone anyway," said Lisa, who felt she had to be brave. With her mother there, she couldn't be a sissy.

The children lay back on their cots. Just as they did, they heard the ghost-sound again. *"OOOOOOOOoooooooo."* The voice carried on the wind. *"OOOOOO-OOOoooooooeeeeeeee,"* it sounded again.

Molly screamed.

Mary Beth pulled her sleeping bag over her head.

Rachel cried.

Lisa got out of bed and crept to the door. She stuck her head out of the tent opening. But she held on to the sides so they did not flap in the wind. "I can't see anything in the dark," said Lisa.

Molly crept to the door beside Lisa.

The creature's loud voice rang out again, "OOOOOO ooooo eeeee!"

This time Tiny woke up and began to bark. The louder the creature's voice got, the louder Tiny barked. After a while he stopped barking. He threw back his head and howled. "Owwwooo!"

Molly was getting mad. She put her head out of the tent door and yelled, "A hex on you! Dumb ghost! Get out of our camp!"

The voice stopped. Tiny stopped howl-ing.

Then the Scouts heard the voice say, "I'm going to get yooooooou."

"That's no wild animal," said Molly. "Animals can't talk."

"But ghosts can," said Lisa.

Now all four Pee Wees were at the door of the tent. As they watched they saw two white figures move in and out of the trees.

"Look!" screamed Rachel. "There are two ghosts!"

"HELLLLLP!" shouted all four girls.

The white shapes billowed in the wind. Their floppy arms waved and they looked as if they were floating!

All of a sudden Tiny dashed through the door and began to chase the ghosts. The girls chased Tiny.

Then the flaps on the other tents burst open and all the Scouts raced out!

They ran through the woods. The ghosts jumped over a creek with Tiny right behind.

Then the ghosts ran toward the camp. It seemed as if they couldn't see where they were going. Soon they bumped smack into the tent that was the kitchen.

Crash went the pots and pans!

Bang! The table toppled over.

Smash! The food fell from the cupboards.

It sounded like glass breaking. Wet things were dripping. By now everyone in the whole camp was awake and chasing the ghosts.

Suddenly a lantern came on, and light filled the kitchen tent.

"Yuck!" said Rachel. "I stepped in maple syrup."

The other Scouts were stepping in food
too. Food was all over. Chairs were on
their sides. The place was a mess.

40

*   *   *

The ghosts were under it all. They were trapped on the floor. Tiny had a foot on one ghost's body. He barked and barked.

"Tiny caught the ghosts!" cried Molly. "Tiny is a hero."

CHAPTER 5
Rat's Knees!

All of a sudden, one ghost started to cry. Mrs. Peters lifted the chairs and cleaned the food off his body. Then she shone the lantern over him.

"My legs are broken!" wailed the ghost. "And that dog walked on my stomach!"

The Scouts stared.

A ghost did not get broken legs, thought Molly. And do they have stomachs? Hey, that voice sounded familiar!

The ghost slowly got to his feet. The other ghost was still moaning.

"He has a sheet on!" said Mrs. Peters.

A real ghost did not wear a sheet, thought Molly. A real ghost was made out of something like smoke. White smoke. Something that was like a cloud. This was no cloud!

Mrs. Ronning marched up and pulled the sheet off of the ghost.

"Sonny Betz!" shouted the Pee Wee Scouts. "It's not a ghost, it's Sonny Betz!"

"Roger made me do it!" he shouted. He pointed to the other ghost.

Some of the Scouts began to laugh. Some of them called him names. "Dumb bunny Sonny!"

Molly did not laugh. Being scared in the woods at night was not funny.

A hex on Sonny Betz.

A hex on Roger White.

A double hex.

Sonny was still sobbing in pain. Mrs. Ronning checked his legs. She felt all his bones. He cried louder. "Nothing is broken," said Mrs. Ronning.

"He made me do it," said Sonny again, pointing.

Mrs. Peters pulled the sheet off the other ghost. Sure enough, it was Roger.

"It was his idea!" Sonny cried. "Roger said we should scare the girls."

Roger did not look hurt. He looked sheepish. He looked as if he would like to dash out the door and run away. "It was just a joke," muttered Roger.

*　　*　　*

Molly felt like giving Roger and Sonny a big smack. Pow! Bang!

But Mrs. Peters said, "I think the ghosts have suffered enough. I hope they learned a lesson. Jokes are dangerous. They could have been hurt."

"This camp is named wrong," said Mary Beth. "Instead of Camp Hide-Away, I think we should call it Camp Ghost-Away!"

"Yeah!" shouted Molly. "That is a good name."

In the morning Mrs. Peters made Roger and Sonny clean up the mess in the kitchen.

Everyone was yawning when they came to breakfast. They had all missed a lot of sleep because of the ghosts. But when the food came, they were hungry.

"Pancakes." said Mary Beth. "I love pancakes."

Rachel said, "I don't eat pancakes. My dad says there's too much sugar in them."

Molly groaned. Rachel was a fussbudget. She just drank orange juice and ate some grapefruit.

Molly made a face at the grapefruit. "Sour," she said. "It gives me the creeps. Yuck!"

"You'll be sorry when all your teeth fall out," said Rachel.

"Teeth-schmeeth," said Molly. "My teeth are as good as yours."

Later that morning, Mrs. Peters said, "Everyone into your swimsuits."

When the Pee Wees were ready, she said, "Let's see if you can learn to float. When you can float alone, you will get the Pee Wee float badge."

47

"You can't float," said Rachel to Molly. "You ate too many pancakes."

Molly wanted to stick out her tongue. She wanted to hex her. She wanted to say a bad word.

All of a sudden she shouted out, "Rat's knees!"

It felt good. It was better than a hex. Rats were ugly things. It was a bad word. And a new one!

When they got to the beach there was a lifeguard. He looked old, maybe eighteen. His name was Rick. He showed them how to do the dead man's float.

"Just relax," said Rick. "Then your body will float."

The Pee Wees tried it. Rick held his arms under each of them at first. Then he let go.

When he let go of Lisa, she floated!

When he let go of Tim, he floated!

But when he let go of Molly, she began to sink. Plunk, plunk, plunk.

Molly's feet sank down. Right down to the bottom of the lake. She could touch even the ground with her toes!

Molly kicked her legs to get them up. She got a big gulp of lake water.

"I can't do it," she sputtered. Then some water went up her nose.

"I told you, you ate too many pancakes!" Rachel said. Rachel could float before she came to camp. She had had private swimming lessons in kindergarten.

Rat's knees! A hex on Rachel.

"Don't worry," said Rick the lifeguard. "It takes time to learn to float. You have to relax all of your muscles."

Molly felt like crying. She even felt

like going home. It was no fun to be a failure. She was as smart as they were. Why couldn't she float? Maybe Rachel was right! She was too fat!

Rachel went to the tent and changed into her other swimsuit.

Molly practiced floating with Rick. But she still sank. Soon it was time to go out in the rowboat. Molly still could not float.

Rick showed them how to row. Sonny tried it. His oars flopped around, but the small rowboat moved.

"Good!" said Rick.

Then Roger rowed. He got water in the boat. The girls got wet.

"Hey, stop it!" said Rachel. "I just got all dried off!"

But Rick said, "Good!"

Then it was Molly's turn.

51

Molly pulled on one oar. Then the other. The oars were heavy. She felt one begin to slip. Ker-plop! One of the oars fell off the boat. It sank to the bottom of the lake as the Pee Wees watched.

Rick did not say Good. He said, "How are we going to get in to shore?" He had to row all the way in with one oar. It took a long time.

"Ho-ho! What a rower!" shouted Roger. He made sounds like the oar going into the water. "Ker-plop, ker-plop." Everyone laughed.

Molly was getting tired of camp. Everyone could learn camp things but her.

After lunch, the Pee Wee Scouts went on a nature hike with Mrs. Peters. They looked for seeds and berries. They listened to the birds sing. Mary Beth found a stone that was an agate. Rachel found a robin's blue eggshell. Tim Noon found a rare wildflower. But Molly got poison ivy.

"Now, everyone, look here," said Mrs. Peters. "Stay away from this plant. It has three leaves together. It looks just like the picture in our nature book."

The Scouts all looked at it closely. "That was dumb," said Rachel. "Why did you touch it?"

"It doesn't look like the picture in the book," muttered Molly. She scratched and scratched.

Mrs. Peters put some lotion on her arms. She still itched. Rat's knees!

6

I Want My Mother

Everyone was tired by suppertime. Everyone but Rachel. She put on a new outfit for supper. It had an anchor on the shirt and a whistle around the neck.

Rachel made a face. "I hate hot dogs!" she said. "I thought we'd have a picnic with steak and stuff."

After supper the Scouts had a treasure hunt. Then they sang around the campfire. They sang the Pee Wee Scout song.

Rachel got ashes and mustard on her new outfit. And Roger pushed her into the lake with her new sandals on.

Camp wasn't so bad after all, thought Molly. Even though her arms were still itching.

Soon it was dark. Everyone helped put the campfire out. All of a sudden there was the sound of someone crying. Molly looked around. Sonny was sitting on a tree stump. Tears were running down his face.

Mrs. Peters went over to him and said, "What's the matter, Sonny? What happened?"

Sonny cried even louder. He buried his face in his hands. Everyone ran over to see why he was crying.

"I want my mother!" screamed Sonny. "I want to go home!"

Mrs. Peters put her arm around Sonny.
"You're just homesick," she said. "You
will feel better in the morning."

"Baby," muttered Rachel. "Mama's boy."

Mrs. Peters tried to make Sonny feel better. She gave him warm milk and tucked him into his sleeping bag. Sonny still sobbed.

"He is really spoiled," said Rachel when they were in bed. "Can't even leave his mother when he's in first grade. Yuck!"

In the middle of the night Sonny came to the girls' tent. He was carrying a blanket and crying. He was not playing ghost now.

"I want to go home!" he screamed.

Mrs. Peters heard the noise and came running.

"I want to go home," wailed Sonny. "Right now!"

All of the Pee Wee Scouts were up now. They wondered what Mrs. Peters would do.

"You should have stayed home," muttered Roger. "Babies shouldn't come to camp."

Sonny wailed louder. "I feel sick," he said, holding his stomach.

"Homesick," said Mrs. Peters. "You are just homesick, Sonny."

"It feels awful," sobbed Sonny.

"I guess the only thing to do is to call Sonny's mother," said Mrs. Peters.

Sonny threw his arms around Mrs. Peters. "Call her!" he cried. "Tell her to come and get me right away!"

Mrs. Peters went up the hill to the campground office to use the telephone. When she came back Sonny was still sobbing.

"Is she coming? Is she coming?" he asked.

"Yes," said Mrs. Peters. "She is leaving right away."

No one could sleep because of all the excitement. "Sonny's mama has to rescue him!" sang Roger.

"Mama's boy, mama's boy," sang Rachel.

"Rat's knees!" said Molly.

At last Sonny's mother came. Sonny leaped into the car and hugged her. "Take me home!" he cried.

Mrs. Betz put her arms around Sonny and hugged him.

The Scouts giggled. Mrs. Betz drank a cup of coffee and then they left.

Finally the camp was settled down for the night.

Molly was almost asleep, when she heard a sound. What was it? She listened closely. Someone else was crying. It was Rachel!

Molly crept over to her cot. "What is the matter with you?"

"I'm homesick too." She sniffed. "I want my mother!"

Suddenly Molly heard something else. It was Mary Beth! She was crying into

60

her pillow too. And so was Lisa! Even
though her mother was close by.

"Rat's knees!" said Molly. "I'm the only
one here who isn't homesick!"

CHAPTER 7

Molly the Brave

The Pee Wee Scouts slept late. When they got up for breakfast they found out that lots of them had been homesick. Tim and Roger had been crying. And two girls in the tent next to Molly's had cried too.

"I guess Molly is the brave one." said Mrs. Peters. "The only one who didn't get homesick!"

"It's not my fault," grumbled Rachel. "My mom said Pee Wee Scouts are pretty young to be gone overnight."

"Homesickness is an awful thing," said Mrs. Peters. "It feels like real sickness. It is nothing to be ashamed of."

"See?" said Rachel to Molly, making a face. Molly made a face back. Molly was still the bravest! She was still the only one who was not homesick. That meant she acted older than six. It meant she was more grown up than the other Pee Wee Scouts.

Molly the brave. Rat's knees! That sounded good.

Rick came to get the Scouts for swimming. Molly still could not float. But when they went rowing, she did not drop the oar in the water. She rowed a little way by herself. But the boat kept turning around in a circle. Rick helped her. He showed her which oar to pull.

*   *   *   *

After lunch the Scouts took naps. Then Mrs. Peters showed them how to weave baskets out of straw. They took their baskets down the road to pick some wild berries. Mrs. Ronning went too.

Rachel had another new camp outfit on. It was bright pink.

Rat's knees! thought Molly. Rachel must be rich. Rachel's gold bracelet sparkled in the sun. Mary Beth's ring sparkled too.

"Is this a berry?" called Roger, holding up something red.

"No, Roger, that isn't a berry we can eat. Be careful to pick only the kind I showed you," said Mrs. Peters.

"What about this?" said Rachel, waving something blue in her hand.

"That is a grape," said Mrs. Peters. "That is all right to pick."

"Don't you know what a *grape* is, dummy?" said Roger.

Rachel made a face. She didn't like to crawl on the ground to get berries. Berries stained. Her new outfit would get dirty. And her hair got all messed up on the twigs and low branches.

Molly had a lot of berries in her basket. She found a patch of red, red strawberries. And a patch of blue, blue blueberries. She would have more berries than anyone!

"I hate these bugs!" shouted Rachel. "They're flying in my eyes!" She waved her arms at the bugs.

"Put some of this on, Rachel," called Mrs. Peters. She handed her a can of bug spray.

"Yuck!" said Rachel. "That makes me smell! It makes my hair ishy! My mom doesn't like me to use that."

"You'll be scratching tonight," said Mrs. Peters. "Mosquitoes bite."

Rat's knees! Rachel should have stayed home, thought Molly. She didn't like the camp food. She didn't like bug spray. She didn't like tents. She was homesick. Rachel Myers was a big baby.

Soon most of the troop's baskets were filled. "Let's start back to camp now," said Mrs. Peters, counting noses.

The Pee Wee Scouts followed Mrs. Peters. They were all scratching. They had berry juice on their arms. They were sunburned too.

When they got back to camp, Mary Beth said, "My ring is lost!"

She held up her hand. Sure enough, the little gold ring was not on her finger.

She had it on when they left to pick berries. Molly had seen it.

"Oh, dear!" said Mrs. Peters. She frowned.

"I'll bet someone stole it," said Rachel.

"No one took it," said Mrs. Peters. "It must have fallen off when we were picking berries."

Mary Beth looked as if she wanted to cry. "It was real gold," she said. "My aunt gave it to me."

"It is best to leave jewelry at home when we camp," said Mrs. Peters. She looked at Rachel's gold bracelet. Rachel put her arm behind her back.

"Don't worry, Mary Beth," said Mrs. Peters. "We will find your ring." Everyone set their baskets down on a camp table and went back to look for Mary Beth's ring. Even Rachel.

* * *

"Rat's knees!" said Molly. "It could be
buried in all this grass."

The Scouts looked everywhere Mary

Beth had been. They looked under leaves. They looked on low branches. They looked in the ditches beside the road. No ring.

Then it began to get dark. They would have to leave it. The Pee Wees were going home tonight.

"Someone will have to drive out and look tomorrow, when it is light," said Mrs. Peters.

Mary Beth was very brave. She looked as if she might cry, but she didn't. She began to sort the berries with the other Scouts.

Suddenly Molly had an idea. She went over to the basket that Mary Beth had used. Molly shook the basket. Sure enough, it made a noise. A noise that berries did not make. Clink, clink, clink!

70

Molly tipped the basket and reached her hand down to the bottom. There was something hard there. Something hard and round and shiny. It was a ring!

"Look!" shouted Molly, running over to Mary Beth. "I found it!"

Now Mary Beth was crying. But they were tears of happiness. She threw her arms around Molly and hugged her.

71

"It must have slipped off my finger when I put berries in the basket," she said. "It is a little bit too big for me."

All the Scouts clapped for Molly. Rat's knees! This was the second fun thing that happened to her at camp! And now it was time to leave. Just when things were getting good.

CHAPTER **8**

Badges

The Pee Wee Scouts fell asleep on the way back to town. They were too tired to sing. They were too tired to talk. Camp had worn them out.

"The park will be boring now," said Lisa.

"But we have Scouts on Tuesday," said Mary Beth. "The day after tomorrow."

Everyone was eager for Tuesday to come. On Tuesday they would get their badges. The donut badges. The swimming badges. The rowing badges. The nature badges. All the camp badges!

But Molly had no badge to wait for. She had not sold one hundred donuts. She could not float. She could not row. She did not find a rock or a wildflower.

When Tuesday came around, the Pee Wees met at Mrs. Peters's house. It will be boring to watch the others get badges, thought Molly. She sat on the floor and

pretended to be snoring. Boring, boring, boring. Snoring boring.

"Now!" said Mrs. Peters loudly. "What did you like best about camp?"

"Swimming!" said Rachel.

"Rowing!" said Lisa.

"Being a ghost!" said Roger.

"Finding my ring," said Mary Beth.

Molly wished Mrs. Peters would give out the badges. She wanted to get it over with. Finally Mrs. Peters held up a pile of badges. All the Scouts cheered. Except Molly.

"The first badge," said Mrs. Peters, "is for selling the most donuts. We all know who gets that badge! Rachel and Sonny are tied for first place, and Roger comes in second."

Rachel and Sonny went up to get their badges. Then Roger went up. Everyone clapped. A hex on them, thought Molly. And a hex on donuts.

Sonny's mother clapped loudly. She was the only mother at the meeting. Baby Sonny. Homesick Sonny. Rat's knees!

Mrs. Peters called Tim Noon for the nature badge. She called Rachel and Mary Beth for the swimming badge. And Roger got a badge for rowing.

Soon almost everyone had a badge. Or two or three. Molly was not bored anymore. She was hurt. She felt left out. She was the only one who did not get any badge at all.

Molly felt a tear start to roll down her cheek. Oh, no, she thought, I don't want to cry.

"Molly Duff!" called Mrs. Peters.

Molly sat up.

"Come up," said Mrs. Peters. "I have a badge for you."

Molly wondered what badge she could

get. She had not earned any. But she got up and walked to the front of the room.

"This is a new badge," Mrs. Peters said. "Just for Molly. I made it up specially for her. It's the 'I didn't get homesick' badge!"

Mrs. Peters pinned the badge on Molly's blouse. Everyone clapped. Molly grinned. She wasn't bored now. Or hurt.

"And I have one more," said Mrs. Peters. "This is specially for Molly too. She is the only one at camp who earned this badge. And it is an important one."

She pinned another badge on Molly's blouse. It was a "finder's badge."

"Finding Mary Beth's ring deserves a badge," said Mrs. Peters.

The Pee Wee Scouts clapped again. Molly had been last, but she wasn't least.

It was true she could not float. And she could not row very well. But she did find the ring. And she was the only one at camp who was not homesick!

Rat's knees! she thought. Why can't Pee Wee camp last all summer!

♪ ♪ Pee Wee Scout Song ♪ ♪
(to the tune of
"Old MacDonald Had a Farm")

Scouts are helpers, Scouts have fun,
Pee Wee, Pee Wee Scouts!
We sing and play when work is done,
Pee Wee, Pee Wee Scouts!

With a good deed here,
And an errand there,
Here a hand, there a hand,
Everywhere a good hand.

Scouts are helpers, Scouts have fun,
Pee Wee, Pee Wee Scouts!

✭ Pee Wee Scout Pledge ✭

We love our country
And our home,
Our school and neighbors too.

As Pee Wee Scouts
We pledge our best
In everything we do.